A Cub Explores

By Pamela Love
Illustrated by Shannon Sycks

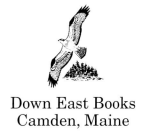

Down East Books
Camden, Maine

Text © 2003 by Pamela Love
Illustrations © by Shannon Sycks

Cover and interior design by Lindy Gifford

Printed in China

6   5   4   3   2   1

ISBN 0-89272-593-1

Library of Congress Control Number 2003115152

DOWN EAST BOOKS
Camden, Maine
A division of Down East Enterprise, publishers of Down
East *magazine, www.downeast.com*

For catalog information and book orders, visit
www.downeastbooks.com, or call 800-685-7962

One late summer afternoon, two black
bears went walking in a shallow brook.
To cool off, the mother bear stopped to roll.

Her cub splashed along much farther downstream. Every now and then he tried to trap a fish, with no luck.

Finally, the mother bear stood, shook hard, and ambled up the bank.

But the cub was in no hurry to leave the water. Now he was turning over rocks with his paws. His mother often did that on dry land to find insects to eat.

One stone puzzled him. The cub sniffed it, flipping it over and back again. It didn't smell or feel like the other rocks. But before he could satisfy his curiosity, an annoyed mother-bear *Huff!* reminded him to follow.

As he scrambled uphill, a head and
four legs popped out of the "stone,"
which was really a shell. Quickly,
the painted turtle swam off.

The mother led her cub to some
newly ripened blackberries.
Neatly, she slurped up the fruit.

The cub didn't have her skill yet. Sweet juice soon stained his paws and muzzle. Once he'd stripped off the berries he could reach, the cub squeezed forward to look for more.

He'd gone farther than he realized when the wind changed direction. He sniffed. Something was coming.

His mother sensed it too. She growled as she came up behind the cub. That signal meant "Danger!"

The cub ran straight to a nearby pine. His claws scrabbled on its bark as he climbed to safety.

A bull moose was approaching, striding powerfully through the brush.

For a moment the mother bear stared at him. His hooves and antlers made him dangerous. But with her cub safely away, there was no reason to fight, so she loped off to rejoin him.

Meanwhile, the cub had sensed something unusual in the branches above him. He sniffed again. Yes, there was definitely *something* up there. Something unfamiliar, not a squirrel or a bird. Curious, he climbed higher to take a look.

Snarl! The cub was face to face with a mother bobcat. She blocked the way while her two kittens scrambled to higher branches. They turned to hiss and spit at the cub.

Puzzled, the cub reached out with one paw only to have the bobcat lash out, smacking it aside with one of hers. The cub was frightened. Trees had always been safe before. He clambered down as quickly as he could, bawling for his mother.

When he reached the forest floor, he raced off.
He stopped only when he collided with something big—his mother.

The cub was more frightened than hurt by
the bobcat's claws. He cuddled against his
mother and nursed. Soon he felt much better.

They moved on. The mother foraged here and there, digging up roots and choosing safe mushrooms. The cub watched her closely. Next year he'd need to find his own food.

But sometimes he was bored. Then he nibbled on a stick or chased his tail. Once he climbed on his mother's back and slid off.

At sunset, the two bears headed for a spruce in which to spend the night. On the way, the cub noticed a birch falling down at the edge of a nearby pond. What were those strange animals moving around the toppled tree? He stood for a better view, and sniffed. He still didn't know what they were.

Lagging behind his mother, the cub sneaked off for a closer look. Softly, he padded toward them.

Splash! Splash! The beavers dove into the pond. *Smack! Smack!* They slapped their tails hard to warn others. Beavers know that bears can be trouble.

In daylight, the cub *might* have investigated. But at dusk, the two very loud sounds were enough to frighten him back to his mother.

She was waiting patiently beneath
the spruce. She followed the cub
into its branches and nestled
beside him. Together, they yawned.

There would be time for more
exploring in the morning.

Some Questions and Answers About American Black Bears

• What color is an American black bear? If you guessed black, you're right . . . but if you picked brown, grayish-blue, cinnamon, or white, you wouldn't be wrong! Black bears come in all these colors. For some reason, the closer the bear is to the Atlantic Ocean, the more likely it is to be black; the closer to the Pacific, one of the other colors. Also, some black bears have a white splotch on their necks or chests.

• Where do American black bears live? Mostly in the United States (except Hawaii) and Canada, with a few in Mexico. In the U.S., they are most common in the northern and western states.

• What do black bears eat? Almost anything! That includes plants, berries, nuts, insects (a bear eating from a hive wants the honey *and* the bees), eggs, and meat.

• What can bear cubs do better than adult bears? Climb trees! Since they are lighter than adults, they can climb onto smaller and higher branches. A black bear cub will go up whenever it's frightened, but it will also climb looking for a place to sleep or food.

• When are bear cubs born? During the winter. As sleepy as she is, the mother bear nurses her cubs, licks them to keep them clean, curls around them to keep them warm, and protects them from any animals who might try to hurt them. All bears are dangerous, but mother bears are the most dangerous of all. No one should ever go near a wild bear cub.